WHEN THE SUN FORGOT TO RISE

WRITTEN
BY
TAHIR
SHAH

DRAWN BY
ALEX
CRAMPTON

WHEN THE SUN FORGOT TO RISE

Secretum Mundi Publishing Ltd
Kemp House
City Road
London
EC1V 2NX
United Kingdom
www.secretum-mundi.com
info@secretum-mundi.com

First published by Secretum Mundi Publishing Ltd, 2022

WHEN THE SUN FORGOT TO RISE

VERSION 08022022

TEXT © TAHIR SHAH
ILLUSTRATIONS © ALEX CRAMPTON

Tahir Shah asserts the right to be identified as the Author of the Work
in accordance with the Copyright, Designs and Patents Act 1988.
A CIP catalogue record for this title is available from the British Library.

Visit the author's website at: www.tahirshah.com

ISBN: 978-1-914960-22-2

This book is for Lily,
who is such an inspiration to us all.

Once upon a time…

    the herds of reindeer were so vast

        that when spied from the heavens

            by the great eagles of the frozen plains,

                they looked like ants.

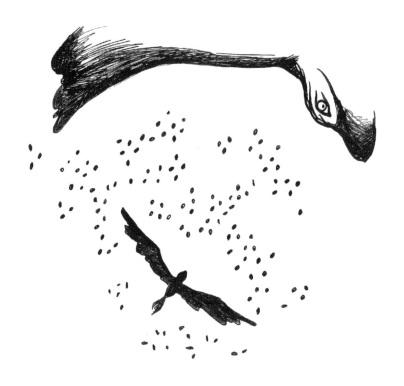

The ground was so thick with ice that only the hardiest creatures survived the winter.

And as for human communities...

...they

were

few

and

far

between.

No

one

with

any

sense

would

endure

what

was

known

by

one

and

all

as

'The

Great

Darkness'.

Months passed…

…in which there was almost no sunlight.

(A DISTINCT
ABSENCE
OF
SUN)

As one night slipped into the next, the people who

endured the unendurable

…would huddle together and tell tales.

Or rather, they would tell a single tale

    which roamed on and on,

        as endless as the arctic tundra

            beyond the wooden walls of the homestead.

Passed down from one
generation to the next,
the tale was sacred
because it contained
the collected wisdom
of the tribe.

Once

it

had

been

told

from

beginning

to

end,

the

first

strains

of

sunlight

would

break

out

across

the

horizon.

Such was the length

of the story – which

was called the

'The Tale of Elypsia'

– that only the elders

of the community

were permitted

to recount it…

...for

only

they

had

committed

to

memory

the

many

twists

and

turns,

and

all

the

details

that

were

so

central

to

the

narrative.

Of all the elders, the finest at recounting
The Tale of Elypsia was an old crone.

She could remember the 'endless freezing', and the
summer long, long ago when the great mountains thawed.

She

knew

that

her

memory

was

fading

faster

than

fast…

and

that

she

would

soon

forget

the

tale.

Day after day

she spoke the story

through the darkness.

And, as she did so,

the next generation listened well,

and they listened hard…

…because they knew that soon
they would be required to pass
on the tale as faultlessly to the
youngers as had been done for them.

At last, her energy drained, her mind fading, the elder spoke the final sentence in a voice so frail it was barely heard at all:

'And then the queen drank the last of the mead, climbed onto her sleigh, and raced towards the sunrise.'

Everyone in the homestead, who had listened through the dark days and nights, applauded.

MORE!! MORE! HURRAH!!!
BRAVO!! CLAP! CLAP! CLAP! Wonderful! Just wonderful!!

When the cheers had waned, one of the children, a little girl called Floria, ran to the window.

Wiping away the ice that caked the glass, she peered out into the curtain of black that shrouded the world in which they lived.

'The dawn should be here by now!' Floria cried.
'It's supposed to be bright when
The Tale of Elypsia ends.'

The

    child's

        father

            touched

                a

                    fingertip

                        to

                            his

                                chin.

'Perhaps we finished a little earlier than usual this year,' he said with a smile.

'Let's wait until tomorrow,' Floria's mother said. 'It's sure to get light then.'

So

Floria,

and

all

the

others,

waited.

They waited…

…and

they waited.

And

    they waited,

        and they waited.

They

waited

a

night…

…and

then

a

day…

…and they waited a week…

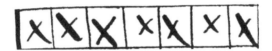

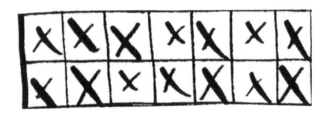

...and then a pair of weeks.

After that, they waited an entire month….

…and more.

But still, sunrise did not come.

Worried what effect the lack of sunlight would have on the herd,

Floria's father touched a fingertip to his chin once again.

'I wonder what could have happened,' he said.

Floria
stared
hard
into
her
father's
eyes.

'It's obvious,' she said. 'The sun has been asleep for so long that she's forgotten to rise.'

There was laughter as everyone enjoyed the words of the child.

When the laughter was over and silence prevailed,

Floria spoke once again: 'Tomorrow I am going to

venture out into the darkness,' she said,

'and I'm going to remind the sun to rise!'

Again…

…there was laughter.

And
again,
everyone
enjoyed
the
words
of
the
child.

Next morning, Floria was up long before her brothers and sisters. Slipping on her clothes, she went to the window…

...and brushed off the ice.

Amazingly,

it

seemed

even

darker

than

before.

With her parents and all the other children still asleep,
Floria put on her heavy coat and went to the door.

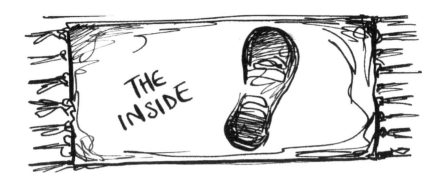

Then, feeling braver than she had ever felt before…

…she slipped outside.

The darkness was so gloomy that the little girl could hardly see where she was going. But gradually, her eyes became accustomed to the darkness.

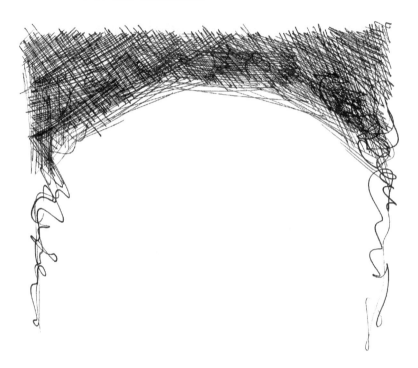

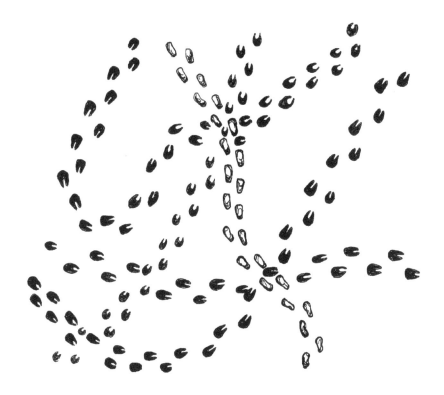

Weaving through the herd of reindeer, she made her way out from the encampment into the arctic wasteland that lay beyond.

As she walked, she told herself fragments of the story,
The Tale of Elypsia, which she had listened to throughout
the winter.

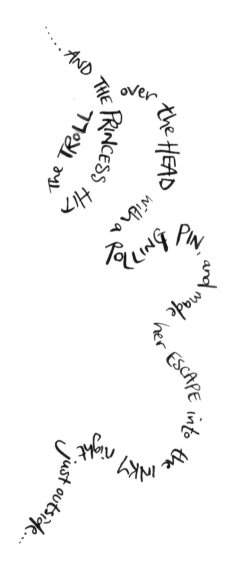

...AND THE PRINCESS HIT THE TROLL over the HEAD with a ROLLING PIN, and made her ESCAPE into the INKY night, just outside...

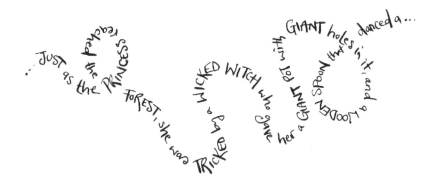

... Just as the PRINCESS (probably) even the FOREST, she was TRICKED by a WICKED WITCH who gave her a GIANT POT with a GIANT holes in it, and a WOODEN SPOON that danced a ...

'One day,' she told herself, 'I will speak the tale better than it has ever been spoken. And when I do, the naughty little sun won't dare stay asleep as she has done. It's not respectful! When I get to her, I'll give her a firm telling-off!'

All morning, Floria paced towards the end of the tundra, her boots scraping against the ice, her face frozen.

She might have wished she had stayed at home in the warmth, but The Tale of Elypsia kept her going, as did the thought of scolding the sun.

Hours after leaving the homestead, Floria began to wonder where the sun could be. After all, it wasn't as though she could be hiding in a cleft in the rocks, or beneath a blanket of ice and snow.

However far Floria walked, she couldn't get to the end of the land… to where the next horizon lay.

It was then that she had an idea.

Marching out in search of the sun was showing weakness.

If she was strong – a fearless little girl who wasn't afraid of scolding the sun – she would surely want the sun to come to her, rather than the other way around.

So, digging her heels into the ice,

she refused to take another footstep.

FIRMLY
DUG IN

Then, rubbing a hand to her chest to warm up her lungs,
she yelled:

'You're a very, very naughty little sun, and you're to
wake up at once! If you don't, I'll get very angry with you!
Do you hear me?!'

Silence.

Silence… but for the distant roar of an avalanche.

So Floria yelled a second time, far louder and more stridently than before.

But again, there was silence…

…except

for

one

of

the

reindeer

calling

out

far

away.

Her heels still dug deep into the ice, Floria thought long and hard.

'If I was a naughty little sun that had fallen fast asleep,' she said to herself, 'what would it take to wake me?'

Thinking harder than she had ever thought of anything before, she thought of how her mother and father would beg her to get up on the deepest, darkest winter mornings…

…and how she would want to stay in bed…

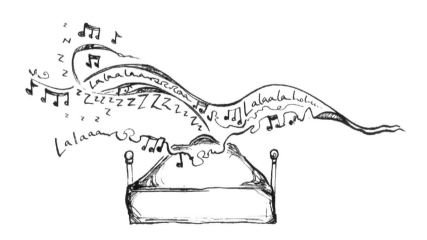

The

only

way

she

would

agree

to

get

up

snug

her

out   of   little

bed

was

when

her

mother

sang

to

her.

'That's

what I'll

do,' Floria

said to her

herself,

'I'll sing

the sun

awake!'

So, filling her lungs once again with frozen morning air,
she sang and she sang…

...and

she

sang

and

she

sang.

She

sang

of

birds,

of

forests,

and

of

rivers…

…and

she

sang

of

little

chicks…

...of

mountains,

and

of

eagles

soaring

high

in

the

summer

sky.

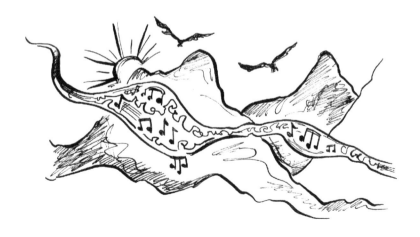

And, as she sang, something remarkable happened…

The faintest rays of sunlight warmed against the night sky and slowly began to break across the horizon.

Still Floria sang, her young voice charming
the stream of light.

By now, the sunshine was so dazzling...

...that Floria took off her mittens and warmed her hands until they were roasting.

Having jumped up and down with delight,
she remembered her manners...

She called out to the horizon, adorned with a glowing aura of gold, yelling:

'Thank you, dearest sun, for waking from your slumber, and for bringing beauty to our world! Every day that you shine above me, I'll thank you as I'm doing now. And, when you go to sleep again after working so hard through weeks and months, I'll remember to wake you. So don't worry about oversleeping, if it ever happens again!'

Then, her short little body throwing out the longest of shadows, Floria tramped home…

…to tell her family how it had been her singing that had woken up the sun.

finis

Timbuctoo

Midas

Zigzagzone

Nasrudin

Travels With Nasrudin

The Misadventures of the Mystifying Nasrudin

The Peregrinations of the Perplexing Nasrudin

The Voyages and Vicissitudes of Nasrudin

Nasrudin in the Land of Fools

Stories

The Arabian Nights Adventures

Scorpion Soup

Tales Told to a Melon

The Afghan Notebook

The Man Who Found Himself

The Caravanserai Stories

Ghoul Brothers

Hourglass

Imaginist

Jinn's Treasure

Jinnlore

Mellified Man

Skeleton Island

Wellspring

When the Sun Forgot to Rise

Outrunning the Reaper

The Cap of Invisibility

On Backgammon Time

The Wondrous Seed

The Paradise Tree

Mouse House

The Old Wind

The Treasury of Tales

The Mysterious Musings of Clementine Fogg

Miscellaneous

The Reason to Write

Zigzag Think

Being Myself

Research

Cultural Research

The Middle East Bedside Book

Three Essays

Lightning Source UK Ltd.
Milton Keynes UK
UKHW012036060223
416577UK00004B/558/J